Acting Edition

I0687894

Men Are Dogs

by Joe Simonelli

SAMUEL FRENCH

No one shall make any changes in this title(s) for the purpose of production. No part of this book may be reproduced, stored in a retrieval system, scanned, uploaded, or transmitted in any form, by any means, now known or yet to be invented, including mechanical, electronic, digital, photocopying, recording, videotaping, or otherwise, without the prior written permission of the publisher. No one shall share this title(s), or any part of this title(s), through any social media or file hosting websites.

For all inquiries regarding motion picture, television, online/digital and other media rights, please contact Concord Theatricals Corp.

MUSIC AND THIRD-PARTY MATERIALS USE NOTE

Licensees are solely responsible for obtaining formal written permission from copyright owners to use copyrighted music and/or other copyrighted third-party materials (e.g., artworks, logos) in the performance of this play and are strongly cautioned to do so. If no such permission is obtained by the licensee, then the licensee must use only original music and materials that the licensee owns and controls. Licensees are solely responsible and liable for clearances of all third-party copyrighted materials, including without limitation music, and shall indemnify the copyright owners of the play(s) and their licensing agent, Concord Theatricals Corp., against any costs, expenses, losses and liabilities arising from the use of such copyrighted third-party materials by licensees. For music, please contact the appropriate music licensing authority in your territory for the rights to any incidental music.

IMPORTANT BILLING AND CREDIT REQUIREMENTS

If you have obtained performance rights to this title, please refer to your licensing agreement for important billing and credit requirements.

CHARACTERS

CECILIA MONAHAN – 40-50, therapist
BOB CROWLEY – 40-50, postal delivery man
ROSE MONAHAN – 65-75, Cecelia's mother
TONY RUMSON – 30-50, actor/bartender
ALLISON TAYLOR – 25-35, hair dresser
MADELINE WEINBERG – 30-55, literary agent
JANE RUDOLPH – 30-55, nurse
LORETTA MORRIS – 40-60, secretary

SETTING

The action takes place in the converted "home" office of
Doctor Cecilia Monahan

AUTHOR'S NOTE

Special thanks to Joe Bagnole and Starburst Productions for allowing me the opportunity to showcase my work at The First Avenue Playhouse in Atlantic Highlands, New Jersey. Also thanks to Lori Jean Sigrist, muse extraordinaire! And my children Nicholas, Kristen and Michael.

To my children: Nicholas, Kristen and Michael.
Always follow your dreams and persevere.

ACT I

Scene One

(The home office of **CECELIA MONAHAN**. *A desk is stage right. A couch is center and two chairs and a small table to be used in role playing are back left. Also present is a bookcase with cabinets underneath. A small table is set against the back wall on which sits a pitcher of water and two glasses. A vent leading to the laundry room is apparent on down right wall. One main door leading outside is stage left, another door which leads to the rest of the house is back right. A small air vent is apparent on a wall back right.)*

(Ar rise: **CECELIA** *is sitting at her desk on her cellphone.)*

CECELIA. *(into phone)* No Mother, I'm not bringing anyone to the party next month. *(pause)* That nice Harvey Frankel turned out to be a creep just like the rest of them. *(pause)* I'm sorry Mom, I apologize for my husband dying and for not giving you any grandchildren, but if you're still holding out for that all I can say is that I'm getting a little long in the tooth. *(pause)* No, I don't want Paula to set me up with her dentist! I'm perfectly capable of meeting men on my own, I don't need my little sister to fix me up. Besides, I've heard stories about Dr. Cambell. *(pause)* Like he's another *(pause)* pretentious jerk with a mid-life crisis who left his wife and kids to buy a Porsche convertible, an electric guitar and a hairpiece! *(sarcasm)* You're right, Mom, nobody's perfect. *(pause)*

Yes, my neck is still bothering me a little…stress prob-ably. *(impatiently, as she listens to more unsolicited advice)* Yes Mother…yes Mother…Mom, the only pain in my neck right now is on the phone with me!... *(phone on her desk rings)* I have to go, I have another call coming in, we'll discuss this later. When later? Well since you moved in upstairs I'd venture to guess soon. Goodbye Mom!

(She picks up cordless desk phone.)

Hello Doctor Monahan. Oh hello, Ruth, how are things at the employment agency. *(pause)* You have someone? Great, what's his name? *(She writes on her pad.)* Tony Rumson. Does he have any acting experience? Bartender, huh. Close enough. *(She stands and comes around front of desk.)* Can you send him over around one thirty? Yes, I hope he works out better than the last guy, too. Bye, Ruth.

(Knock at the door... **CECELIA** *is still holding phone.)*

Come in.

(BOB CROWLEY, *a postal delivery man, enters holding a package.)*

BOB. Hi, I've got a delivery for a C. Monahan. Would that be you?

CECELIA. Yes it would. But where's Sarah? She's been delivering my packages for years.

BOB. She's away for a few weeks with the Army Reserves, I'm filling in...My name's Bob. *(He looks around the office.)* Nice office you've got here. Did it come with the house or did you design it yourself?

CECELIA. Pretty inquisitive, aren't you? If you must know... ah, what did you say your name was again?

BOB. Bob, Bob Crowley.

CECELIA. *(She crosses to front of desk.)* This *was* my den. I converted it to an office.

BOB. You're a doctor, right?

CECELIA. *(She reaches for package.)* Psychologist, how'd you guess?

BOB. *(pulls package away to read label)* Says right here on the package. C. Monahan, PhD.

CECELIA. *(sarcastically as she bends over her desk to check her cell phone)* Very good, most men aren't that observant.

BOB. *(checking her out as she's turned away)* I notice a lot of things.

CECELIA. *(She turns back in time to catch him.)* Well, Bob, it's been a real pleasure meeting you but I have to interview a new patient who's due any minute so if you don't mind...

BOB. Oh, yeah...sorry.

(He turns to leave still carrying the package.)

CECELIA. Ah Bob. *(She holds out her hand.)* Haven't you forgotten something?

BOB. Where are my manners? *(He shakes her hand.)* Pleasure to meet you.

CECELIA. The package Bob. I meant the Package.

BOB. Oh yeah. *(hands her package)* Something you've been expecting?

CECELIA. *(She studies the package.)* Yes, but this isn't it. I'm expecting a book.

BOB. Oh, new research book. Let me guess. Women are from Heaven. Men are from Hell. The new way to cope with relationships in the millennium.

CECELIA. Men are from Hell?

BOB. Yeah, that's a hot title, huh? *(He laughs at his own joke.)* Get it, a hot title.

CECELIA. *(sits behind desk)* You really crack yourself up, don't you?

BOB. Don't mind me. My ex-wife always said I was missing a frontal lobe.

CECELIA. Really? Why was that?

BOB. I guess because I usually say what ever is on my mind without thinking about it first. You see the frontal lobe controls your ability to disseminate information and...

CECELIA. I'm familiar with the function of the frontal lobe, I'm a doctor, remember? So you were married. That thought kind of frightens me.

BOB. Must have frightened my 'ex' too, the wedding reception lasted longer than the marriage.

CECELIA. Why am I not surprised.

BOB. So what book *was* it that you were waiting for? Oh, I'm sorry, it's none of my business. Frontal lobe again.

CECELIA. *(up from behind desk)* Actually I'm waiting for the final draft of a book I wrote.

BOB. You wrote it? Impressive. What's it about?

CECELIA. Guess?

BOB. Relationships?

CECELIA. *(sarcasm)* Very good.

BOB. So what's the title?

CECELIA. Well, I was going to call it *Men are Dogs,* but then that wouldn't be fair to the dogs, would it?

BOB. That's a joke, right?

CECELIA. What do you think?

BOB. I think you don't seem very impartial for a relationship therapist. If I were in your position, I think I'd…

CECELIA. Well, you're not. I think I'm a little bit more qualified on the subject than you are.

BOB. *(slight sarcasm as he heads for door)* You're right. I'm only a deliveryman with an ex-wife and a few kids. What would I know about relationships?

CECELIA. *(trying to escort him out)* Now you've got the picture, Bob.

BOB. *(turns around and crosses back)* Only it seems to me that some of the ancient Indian tribes had it right.

CECELIA. *(exasperated but slightly curious)* How do you mean?

BOB. *(sits on couch)* Some American Indian tribes used to segregate the men and women. The men would live together up in the hills while the women remained below in the valley. The men would come down the hills once in a while to *procreate* while the women stayed in the valley and took care of the children. Great system, huh? Eliminates all the idle chatter. You know, the warrior comes home from being out on the plain and the squaw asks him how his day was. He says, we skinned a few buffalo, massacred some settlers, the usual routine. What's for dinner?

CECELIA. How politically incorrect of you...but tell me, how did you learn so much about Native American culture?

BOB. *(rising from the couch)* I watch a lot of Jeopardy.

CECELIA. Is that so?

(ALLISON TAYLOR *enters as* BOB *moves towards the door.)*

BOB. Looks like the new patient is here. Back to work for me. I'll probably see you tomorrow.

CECELIA. *(sarcasm)* I can't wait.

ALLISON. *(She is a blonde, mid-twenties hair dresser. She is chewing gum. She mistakenly introduces herself to* BOB.*)* Hi, I'm Allison Taylor. I hope I didn't interrupt. I'm your one o'clock appointment.

BOB. She's right there.

(BOB *points her to* CECELIA *as he exits.)*

ALLISON. Hi, I'm Allison Taylor, I'm your one o'clock.

CECELIA. So I heard.

ALLISON. Was that fellow your twelve o'clock?

CECELIA. No, but he probably should be. Please have a seat.

(ALLISON *sits on sofa as* CECELIA *rolls her office chair from behind desk to end of couch and sits on it...)*

CECELIA. *(She refers to notes on yellow pad.)* Let's see, you told me you were a hairdresser, is that correct, Allison?

ALLISON. That's right. "Hair Apparent." That's the name of my salon. I run it with my two sisters.

CECELIA. "Hair Apparent." That's a great play on words. Did you think of the name?

ALLISON. No, my sister Annette did. But what play on words were you referring to?

CECELIA. Play on words, you know, *double entendre.*

ALLISON. *(blank stare as she nods her head as if she gets it)* I don't get it?

CECELIA. It's not important...Now Allison, what is it that's bothering you... *(no response)* Wait, let me guess, your boyfriend?

ALLISON. *(genuinely astonished the doctor knew)* Yeah, how did you know?

CECELIA. After twenty plus years of relationship training you kind of sense it. What's his name?

(She starts to take notes.)

ALLISON. *(dreamily)* Brian.

CECELIA. How long have you been seeing him?

ALLISON. *(gushing)* About six months...three weeks and two, no, *three* days!

CECELIA. Not counting the hours?

ALLISON. *(clueless)* Huh?

CECELIA. So tell me your problem Allison. No wait, let me guess. The first three months were terrific than you started noticing signs, right?

ALLISON. Actually, I started noticing signs after two weeks.

CECELIA. Really. Well, how long had you dated him before you slept with him?

ALLISON & CECELIA. Two weeks.

CECELIA. Okay, so you've been him dating for six months and what happens?

ALLISON. Well, at first it's little things. He used to bring me presents when he came over. Like one time he dragged me into a lingerie shop and bought me the cutest neck ledgee.

CECELIA. Nick ledgee? A new designer label?

ALLISON. Huh? No, it's a style of underwear!

CECELIA. Oh, you mean *negligee.*

ALLISON. Is that how you pronounce it? Well anyway, we used to spend all weekend at my apartment and hardly go out because we were so busy having...well, you get the picture...and now...

CECELIA. He doesn't bring you presents?

ALLISON. Now he brings over a six-pack of beer, some microwave popcorn and he doesn't even stay the night.

CECELIA. Is that so?

ALLISON. But the topper was last month. Do you know what he pulled last month?

CECELIA. Why don't you tell me?

ALLISON. Well, we had a big date planned for a Friday night and the day before he breaks it because all his frat brothers have rented a house down the Jersey Shore and he's spending the weekend with them. That started a huge argument and I stopped talking to him.

CECELIA. Go on.

ALLISON. Well, that Friday afternoon he calls me and he's as sweet as can be. He's already down the shore and tells me he misses me and asked if I would drive down to the shore and join him for dinner. He also asked if I can go by his apartment and pick up a few things that he forgot to bring. So, I swing by his apartment and get his wallet and some clothes then drive two hours to the Jersey shore. After getting a flat tire I finally make it down.

CECELIA. And what happened when you got there?

ALLISON. I walk in the restaurant and he's sitting at a table with his buddies totally trashed.

CECELIA. How could you tell?

ALLISON. *(rising from couch)* He was asleep at the table! His head was face down in a platter of lobster fra diablo. When I called his name and he lifted his head there was a piece of lobster claw hanging out of his nose.

CECELIA. Oh, my!

ALLISON. Then he looks at me and says, *(imitating male voice)* "What the hell are you doing here?" And I say, "Duh... You invited me remember?" And he says, "Can't you see I'm here with my friends, get lost." So I threw the salt shaker at him, tossed his stuff on the floor *(She starts to sob as she sits back on couch.)* and walked out.

*(**CECELIA** passes her a box of tissues and she takes one.)*

ALLISON. Why do men always do this to me, Doctor? Before Brian there was Brad. *(again gushing)* Oh boy was he gorgeous! He swept me off my feet and we really bonded.

CECELIA. And how long did you date him for?

ALLISON. Just the one night. It was a blind date. We had dinner then went dancing then back to my place and everything was so romantic.

CECELIA. And what happened?

ALLISON. He spends the night at my place, gets up the next morning and I offer him some coffee. He goes in my refrigerator to get some milk and I was out, so he said run down to the store and get some.

CECELIA. And?

ALLISON. That's the last time I ever saw him.

CECELIA. Wow!

ALLISON. *(reflective)* And the funny part was that there was a container of cream sitting right on the top shelf of my refrigerator. *(again starting to sob)* I guess milk was easier on his stomach.

*(**CECELIA** hands her another tissue which she takes, then reaches for a second.)*

CECELIA. Come now, Allison, don't tell me your trying to defend his actions? What did you say his name was again? *(She writes the names on her pad.)*

ALLISON. Brad. I dated him after Barry. Of course before them there was Ben and Bud...

CECELIA. Bud, Ben, Brian, Brad, Barry. Allison, aren't you noticing a pattern here?

ALLISON. *(oblivious)* Yeah, all men are jerks.

CECELIA. That's not I'm referring to. Allison, all the men you've dated have names that begin with the letter "B."

ALLISON. *(an epiphany)* Hey, you're right. Wow. You are really good.

CECELIA. Just out of curiosity. What's your father's name?

ALLISON. Oh, I see where you're going with this doctor, and you're way off base, my father's name is *William.*

CECELIA. What does your mother call him?

ALLISON. Bill.

CECELIA. I see.

ALLISON. So what do you think I should do about him doctor?

CECELIA. Who, Barry, Brad or Bill?

ALLISON. Brian! I'm talking about Brian! Bill's my father, remember?

CECELIA. Oh, that's right. Well how long has it been since you've seen him? *(referring to her notes)* Let's see, the restaurant was over a month ago.

ALLISON. Oh, we didn't break up after that. He apologized to me when we woke up the next morning.

CECELIA. You slept with him the same night he humiliated you like that?

ALLISON. Well...yeah. I felt a little guilty about leaving him so suddenly so I went back in the restaurant, and he did look kind of cute with that lobster claw hanging out of his nose. So anyway, I talked things over with my father a little later...

CECELIA. *(exasperated)* You talked to Bill...I mean your father, about your relationship with your boyfriend?

ALLISON. You don't think I should have? But where else would I go for a man's point of view? I don't have any brothers and well, a girl's dad would never steer her wrong.

CECELIA. Allison, as a therapist I can safely say that's it's not healthy to go to your parents about every little problem you're having. Don't you think there comes a time when you have to cut the 'apron strings'?

(**ROSE** *enters from the interior entrance.*)

ROSE. Oh, I'm sorry. I didn't realize you were with someone. *(to* **ALLISON***)* I'm doctor Monahan's mother. I live upstairs with her.

(**CECELIA** *menacingly backs* **ROSE** *out of the room.*)

Just wondering if you were hungry but we can talk later.

(**ROSE** *exits as* **CECELIA** *returns to her seat.*)

CECELIA. I'm sorry about that interruption Allison. Where were we?

ALLISON. *(sarcasm)* Um…cutting the 'apron strings.'

CECELIA. Oh yes! Well I think it may be helpful if you join my weekly support group for women who basically discuss the same issues you're having.

ALLISON. You mean *their* rotten relationships?

CECELIA. Exactly. We meet tomorrow night at seven. Would you like to join us?

ALLISON. *(She rises from couch.)* Sure, why not? It's not like I have anything else to do. I mean, I was going to color Mrs. Edelson's hair, but I guess those gray roots can wait another day. Besides, my sister Audrey can always fill in.

CECELIA. Your sister's name is Audrey. And you're other sister's name?

ALLISON. Annette.

CECELIA. Alright, I'm going to go out on a limb here, but does your mother's name start with the letter A?

ALLISON. Whoa. You must be clairvoyant. Her name is Amanda.

CECELIA. *(deadpan)* You don't say?

ALLISON. But everyone calls her Betty.

CECELIA. Why am I not surprised.

ALLISON. Well, Betty's her middle name. Well, it's really Elizabeth. Amanda Elizabeth Taylor.

CECELIA. Oh, just like the movie star.

ALLISON. What movie star?

CECELIA. Never mind, Allison. *(She rises.)* I'll see you tomorrow at seven.

ALLISON. Right. Tomorrow at seven. Goodbye, doctor.

(She exits as **CECELIA** *picks up a reference book on her desk and begins to page through it.)*

CECELIA. *(to herself)* Father fixation, Father fixation *(knock at the door)* ...ah later. Come in.

*(***TONY RUMSON**, *a smarmy narcissist and ladies man, enters.)*

TONY. Hi, The Employment Agency sent me over. *(impressed with himself)* I'm Tony.

CECELIA. Oh, yes, Mr. Rumson. I was expecting you. *(She sits behind desk.)* Have a seat.

TONY. Thanks, I will. *(He sits.)*

CECELIA. Did you bring a resume?

TONY. *(proud of himself for even having one)* Yes, I did.

CECELIA. May I see it?

TONY. Oh, of course.

(He pulls a crumpled piece of paper from his back pocket and hands it to her.)

CECELIA. *(perusing resume)* Are you married, Mr. Rumson?

TONY. *(Proud that he's unattached and available. God's gift to women)* Deevorced!

CECELIA. I see. *(writes on pad)* Commitment phobic.

TONY. Yeah. The agency told me you were a psychologist.

CECELIA. That's correct, I am.

TONY. That's interesting.

CECELIA. *(She looks at him.)* You appear to be an excellent physical specimen.

TONY. *(checks himself out)* I do.

CECELIA. Do you work out?

TONY. *(flexing his arms)* A little bit when I have time. Why do you ask?

CECELIA. *(She's back to the resume.)* I see you're a part time bartender. You must meet plenty of single women doing that.

TONY. Yeah, and some of them aren't even single!

CECELIA. Such braggadocio.

*(**TONY** doesn't understand the word then, thinking he gets it, looks down at his crotch and back to **CECELIA**.)*

TONY. Can you notice it from there? I mean, all things being equal, I do pretty well with the women.

CECELIA. And modest, too. You must sweep those women off their feet.

TONY. Never get many complaints.

CECELIA. I bet you don't. *(She rises and walks out from behind desk.)* Tell me, Mr. Rumson…are you the athletic type?

TONY. *(laying on the charm)* Please, it's Tony, call me Tony.

CECELIA. *(playing along)* Thanks, I will. And you may call me *(shooting him down and all business)* Dr. Monahan.

TONY. *(ego deflated)* Oh, okay.

CECELIA. Tell me Tony. Did you play any sports in school?

TONY. Football and wrestling in high school. I did a little boxing in community college. *(He mimics throwing some punches.)*

CECELIA. *(She feels his chin.)* Strong jaw. Excellent.

TONY. Say, just what kind of position are you hiring for anyway?

CECELIA. I'm looking for someone to help with a support group I run.

TONY. *(rises and heads for door)* Well. I hardly think I qualify to help with something like that.

CECELIA. *(stopping him)* You're being too modest Tony, if such a thing is possible. Why don't you let me be the judge of that.

TONY. If you say so. *(He sits on couch.)*

CECELIA. Did the employment agency inform you that I pay my people three times the going rate?

TONY. Yes, they did, as a matter of fact. That's why I jumped at the chance for this interview. They said there was an immediate opening.

CECELIA. Oh that there is! Do you have any acting experience Tony?

TONY. A little. Is that important?

CECELIA. Well, the position does require you to interact with other people.

TONY. Oh, you mean like an improv thing?

CECELIA. That's a good way of putting it.

TONY. I think I'd like that. *(trying to impress one more time)* I played Casanova in our high school production.

CECELIA. *(sarcasm)* Really? Such untapped talent. Now Tony, do you mind if I ask you some personal questions?

TONY. Like you haven't already? Go ahead, ask away.

CECELIA. Tell me about your divorce.

TONY. *(up from couch)* My divorce. Gee, Dr. Monahan, is that really necessary? I mean, I know you're a shrink and all but...

CECELIA. If you're not interested in the position Mr. Rumson, I can just have the agency send over another candidate.

TONY. Alright, alright. For the money you're paying, I'll answer whatever question you want...Let's see, my divorce...well, I guess it was the typical story.

CECELIA. *(up from desk)* How long were you married?

TONY. Ten years. No wait, eleven.

CECELIA. You're not certain how long you were married?

TONY. *(chuckling)* I guess that's why I'm divorced.

CECELIA. Continue. You had been married eleven years and what happened? You started to feel unfulfilled, unappreciated right?

TONY. Basically, yeah. It's like I felt I needed some space, you know.

CECELIA. After all, it would have been 'healthier' for the relationship.

TONY. That's it exactly.

(CECELIA now gets in his face and backs him around couch menacingly.)

CECELIA. Never mind that your ex-wife probably worked like an animal to support you while you went to bartending school, or took acting lessons or learned to sky dive or something. After all, what man wants to be held back by a loving, supportive wife when he has so much to offer the world? NO WONDER SHE LEFT YOU!

TONY. *(falling to couch and meekly)* Does that make me a bad person?

CECELIA. What do you think?

TONY. *(up from couch and heading towards door)* I think if I want abuse like this, I'll go back to my ex-wife.

CECELIA. I apologize Tony. I think you're just the person I've been looking for. Can you start tomorrow evening?

TONY. I'm seriously considering it doc.

CECELIA. Excellent. The group meets at seven but we won't get to your part until about seven thirty.

TONY. And what did you say my part was again?

CECELIA. I thought I explained it to you Mr., Rumson. I simply need you to interact with my support group. You know, role play.

TONY. Yeah, but what kind of support group is it exactly?

CECELIA. *(playfully piquing his interest)* It's a divorced and single women's support group, Tony.

TONY. Divorced and single? And I'm the only guy.

CECELIA. That's right.

TONY. I think I'm going to like this.

CECELIA. Yes, I thought you would. I'll see you tomorrow at seven-thirty then?

TONY. You know Tony, spelled backwards, is Y not!

*(**TONY** exits as **ROSE** enters interior door carrying a laundry basket that has a plate of dip on top of the clothes. She places basket on the couch)*

ROSE. Hello Cecelia, is the coast clear?

CECELIA. Yes Mother. And how many times have I reminded you not to interrupt me during business hours?

ROSE. What's the matter, you don't take a lunch break anymore? Here, try this dip. It's a new recipe.

CECELIA. No thanks, Mother. I'm watching my weight.

ROSE. For whom? You never go out.

(She starts folding laundry.)

CECELIA. I'm sorry I'm not a social butterfly like you, Mother, but my work is my priority. Besides, I've been out of circulation so long I wouldn't know where to look.

ROSE. *(sits on couch)* There are plenty of places. How about taking a cooking class?

CECELIA. *(leans on her desk)* Really, a cooking class? To meet men?

ROSE. I'm taking one. How do you think I got this dip recipe? And, as a matter of fact, I met a pretty nice fellow in class. Maybe I'll invite him over tonight and we'll prepare dinner for that support group of yours. I'm thinking beef bourguignon. Don't you keep some sherry down here?

CECELIA. That recipe calls for burgundy.

ROSE. It's not for the sauce. *(She starts to fold clothes.)*

CECELIA. Mother, I agreed to let you move in upstairs after your last marriage broke up only after you promised you would let me have my space and not invade my privacy. Especially during office hours.

ROSE. I'm sorry, sweetheart, I didn't mean to interrupt the *lonely hearts* club.

CECELIA. They're women who need relationship counseling Mother, not lonely hearts.

ROSE. Counseling? In my day we didn't have counseling to deal with men. We just took a valium and hoped for the best.

CECELIA. They need someone to talk to about their relationship problems.

ROSE. Why can't they figure it out for themselves, like I do.

CECELIA. Sure, you're great at relationships, that's why you've been divorced three times.

ROSE. You can't count the last one.

CECELIA. Why not?

ROSE. I only married him for the medical benefits.

CECELIA. Very funny.

ROSE. You know what you're problem is Cecilia?

CECELIA. Yes, I'm looking right at her.

ROSE. You're problem is you expect too much from a relationship.

CECELIA. Oh, and you're the authority?

ROSE. And you give men too much credit for knowing what they want.

CECELIA. And don't you know what they want, Mom?

ROSE. Sure, they want to fool around at first, so do women.

CECELIA. Really, and what do they want after the thrill is gone, companionship?

ROSE. You got me?

CECELIA. *(optional Viennese accent)* Ah hah, Dr. Rose is stumped.

ROSE. Well you're not going to figure it out sitting behind that desk listening to sob stories. Why don't you go on a date, for God's sake? Did you call that dentist?

CECELIA. No, I didn't.

ROSE. When *are* you going to call him?

CECELIA. When I need a root canal.

ROSE. You know your sister said she heard he had big feet.

CECELIA. What?

ROSE. *(stretching a white sock for emphasis)* You know, big feet.

CECELIA. First of all that's an old wives' tale and I could care less how big his... 'foot' is.

ROSE. I hate to see you so lonely and miserable honey.

CECELIA. Why. You're by yourself at the moment and you don't seem to mind it.

ROSE. Me? I'm old, I don't need the aggravation.

CECELIA. That's exactly how I feel.

ROSE. You're not old, you can still enjoy...well, you know, *'relations'*.

CECELIA. The word is 'sex' Mother.

ROSE. *(She smiles.)* Yeah, sex?

CECELIA. Why are you smiling Mother?

ROSE. *(sighs)* Just reminiscing.

CECELIA. Besides, there are other ways a woman can be fulfilled without having a man around.

ROSE. *(up from couch)* Oh that's disgusting. You're talking about that 'auto exotica' aren't you?

CECELIA. The term is auto erotica, Mother, and that is not what I was referring to, although there's certainly nothing wrong with it. Don't tell me you've never tried it?

ROSE. In my day we never did such a thing. We played tennis, ran around the block, did the dishes...you know, we subjugated.

CECELIA. The word is *sublimated.*

ROSE. You weren't married to your father. We subjugated...

CECELIA. As you said, exercise can be a very capable substitute for sex in some... *(She grabs her shoulder.)* ohhh.

ROSE. What's the matter?

CECELIA. My neck is still a little stiff, I guess.

ROSE. Come sit here, let me help.

(**CECELIA** *sits on the couch as* **ROSE** *crosses behind her and starts massaging her neck.)*

ROSE. *(as she massages)* And I say running a marathon is no substitution for a good roll in the hay.

CECELIA. Mom, an endorphin rush is an endorphin rush.

ROSE. A what rush?

CECELIA. Endorphin…Endorphin. It's a feeling of euphoria…

ROSE. I still say it's not the same as… *(She smiles.)* well, you know…

CECELIA. Having an orgasm, Mother?

ROSE. *(stops massaging)* Not at the moment.

CECELIA. I wasn't asking if you were having one now! I was referring to the concept.

ROSE. *(massages a little more vigorously)* Of what?

(BOB re-enters carrying a package and stands in doorway unnoticed.)

CECELIA. *(exasperated)* An orgasm, ORGASM, ORGASM!

BOB. Is this a bad time?

CECELIA. *(jumps up from couch)* Oh. Hello, Mr. Crowley. I was just having an orgasm..I mean *conversation,* with my mother. *(to* **ROSE***)* Mr. Crowley is our new delivery man.

ROSE. *(crossing between* **CECELIA** *and* **BOB***)* Really? Do you drive one of those brown trucks? Do you have a girlfriend? Answer the second question first.

BOB. No, I don't have a girlfriend, and I don't drive one of those brown trucks.

ROSE. *(to* **CECELIA** *as she looks at* **BOB***'s feet and gestures)* No girlfriend. *(to* **BOB***)* Why no girlfriend?

CECELIA. Mother, really, you're invading Mr. Crowley's privacy.

BOB. It's okay, Dr. Monahan, I don't mind. *(to* **ROSE***)* I guess I'm just too busy for a girlfriend.

ROSE. Oh. *(covering her bases)* You don't have a boyfriend do you?

CECELIA. Mother! *(changing the subject)* Was there something you wanted to give me, Bob?

BOB. *(taking it the wrong way)* Well, I hardly know you, but maybe if we have a few drinks, some dinner perhaps…

CECELIA. I was talking about the package!

ROSE. *(hand gesture)* So was he.

BOB. Oh, yeah. I'm sorry. I think this might be the book you were waiting for. I noticed it behind a shelf in the truck and I knew you were looking forward to reading it so I...

(**ROSE** *takes* **BOB** *by the arm and bringing him towards* **CECELIA.**)

ROSE. So you made a special trip back just to deliver it! Wasn't that thoughtful.

BOB. It's part of the service, Dr. Monahan.

ROSE. *(Pulling* **CECELIA** *closer, she takes the package.)* Please, call her Cecelia.

CECELIA. Mom...

ROSE. *(now close between them with an arm around both)* You know it's a shame two nice single people such as yourselves can't find other nice people to spend time with. I've been trying to encourage Cecelia to call this nice single dentist we know with *big feet!*

CECELIA. Mother!

BOB. *(breaks away)* I think it's time for me to leave.

ROSE. *(pulling him back)* No, stay.

CECELIA. *(frustrated)* Yes, stay, Bob. You and my mother can have a nice eccentric, conversation while I take my manuscript upstairs, run a nice hot bath, and go over my notes, alone and read it in peace.

(She exits interior door.)

ROSE. Don't mind her, Bob, (**ROSE** *pushes* **BOB** *to couch and sits with the laundry basket between them.)* she's just a little high strung. Just like her father, that bum.

BOB. I see.

ROSE. *(She starts to fold laundry again.)* I'm sorry, I didn't mean to say that. It's after what he did to us...

BOB. Broken home, huh?

ROSE. He ran out on me when Cecelia and her sister were babies.

*(She tosses **BOB** a towel to fold.)*

BOB. That must have been tough.

ROSE. I had to go back to work. And this was in the days before daycare. My mother had to watch the girls until they were old enough for school.

BOB. *(continuing to fold laundry)* Well did he at least give you financial support?

ROSE. When he could. He used to drop by once in a while after a gig to see the girls.

BOB. Oh, musician, huh?

*(**BOB** pulls an extra large, brightly colored brassiere from the basket.)*

ROSE. More like a gypsy. But at least he was in the union, so we got some benefits. You know, medical, dental.

BOB. Yeah, a union usually has a good family plan.

ROSE. We were on the *dysfunctional* family plan...but enough about the past. We should just think about today, right?

BOB. Sounds like a good philosophy to me. Carpe Diem!

ROSE. *(stops folding and very impressed)* Oh, you speak French, how nice.

BOB. Actually it's Latin. Carpe Diem. It means *seize the day*, Mrs. Monahan.

ROSE. *(flirting)* Please, call me Rose.

BOB. Okay Rose.

ROSE. *(flirting)* So tell me, Bobby, do you go for older women?

BOB. Not really, Rose, but if I did...

ROSE. Oh too bad... so what do you think of Cecelia?

BOB. You want an honest answer, Rose?

ROSE. Nah, just lie and flatter me.

BOB. In that case, I think she's pretty hot stuff, just like her mother.

ROSE. Really?

BOB. Really.

ROSE. So then, why don't you ask her out?

BOB. Oh, I hardly think I'm her type.

ROSE. Nonsense. I know Cecelia. I know what she likes.

BOB. Really? So are you going to tell me?

ROSE. I'm not sure I should.

BOB. Why not?

ROSE. I'm not sure about you yet. Cecelia may seem like she has things together but she also has a fragile side. She's been hurt before.

BOB. Well, we've all been hurt before, Rose. It's part of life.

ROSE. I guess you're right.

(She rises from couch and **BOB** *follows.)*

Well, you just keep delivering her things she likes and maybe she'll warm up to you, if you get my meaning.

BOB. I'm not sure I do.

ROSE. Women like to be surprised Bob, that's what I mean.

BOB. I'll keep it in mind Rose. Well, I've got to get back to my route. Maybe I'll see you tomorrow. *(He crosses to front door.)* Remember, Carpe Diem!

(He exits as **ROSE** *picks up laundry basket and plate of dip and crosses to interior door.)*

ROSE. Carpe Diem.

(blackout)

Scene Two

(Setting: **CECELIA***'s office – the next evening.)*

(At rise: **MADELINE** *and* **JANE** *are sitting on couch. They each have pillows on there laps and punch them when they are angry.)*

MADELINE. *(swooning)* So, it's our third date, we're curled up on the couch at his place watching a DVD of *Gone with the Wind.* Rhett is about to carry Scarlett up that huge staircase for a little *action* when George plants the longest, most sensual kiss I've ever received, square on my face. Then he turns to me and says, "I know we've only known each other a short time, but there's something I really want to show you. I have it right here in my desk drawer. I think it's something you're going to like."

JANE. *(excited)* Wow, how exciting. What was it? A card?

*(***MADELINE** *shakes her head.)*

Box of candy?

MADELINE. NOPE.

JANE. A gold Bracelet?!

MADELINE. *(venom)* A manuscript.

JANE. Another manuscript?

MADELINE. Third one this year.

JANE. I thought you stopped telling your dates that you were a literary agent.

MADELINE. Somehow they find out. *(She picks up pillow.)* Do you know how that feels? *(She starts punching her pillow.)* It's like me trying to date one of the Steinbrenners because I want to play third base for the Yankees.

JANE. You think it's any better where I work? *(punches her pillow)* I'm a nurse and every guy I date wants a sponge bath and a scrotal exam! At least if the manuscript they give you is good, you can get a new client out of it.

MADELINE. *(grabbing the bottom of* **JANE***'s pillow)* At least you have them by the balls.

(**JANE** *pulls out a paperback book and hands it to* **MADELINE**.)

JANE. Maybe this will help. It's the latest book by that women's relationship therapist, Delores Knight Robinson. Have you read any of her books?

MADELINE. All of them, I'm her agent. *What Women Think, What Men Think, What Men Think Woman Think.*

JANE. *What Men Think Woman Think Men Think.*

MADELINE. That was a good one!

JANE. I hope it works for someone. Those self-help books haven't done me any good.

MADELINE. Tell me about it. We could read every self-help book in print, and we'd still wind up in therapy.

(**ALLISON** *enters from main door.*)

ALLISON. Hello. I'm Allison Taylor. I'm here to join the support group.

(*They all stand and shake hands.*)

JANE. I'm Jane Rudolf and this is Madeline Weinberg.

MADELINE. A pleasure to meet you.

ALLISON. Where's Doctor Monahan?

MADELINE. She'll be down shortly. I think she's having a little *domestic* issue.

ALLISON. Is this the whole group? Just the three of us?

JANE. Oh my, no, Loretta should be here any minute. She works for a slave-driver who keeps her locked up at that desk from nine to five-thirty every day. The she has to rush across town to get here.

MADELINE. She told me she has to eat lunch at her desk, ask permission to go to the bathroom, and sneak outside to have a smoke.

ALLISON. Really? What's her occupation?

JANE. Assistant to a stress therapist.

(**LORETTA**, *the alpha female of the group, enters carrying shopping bag.*)

LORETTA. Hi, everyone. Sorry I'm late. Traffic was a bitch.

MADELINE. Loretta Morris, Allison Taylor.

ALLISON. *(extending hand)* Pleased to meet you.

LORETTA. *(dismissive of* **ALLISON**, *does not shake her hand)* Yeah right. *(to others)* Do you know what that bastard did to me today?!

ALLISON. Who, the slave driver?

> (**LORETTA** *shoots* **ALLISON** *a skeptical glance.)*

MADELINE. We told her about your boss.

LORETTA. *(to* **ALLISON***)* No, not that bastard. *(to others)* "That" bastard.

JANE. She means Frank, her boyfriend. He is still your boyfriend, isn't he?

LORETTA. Who knows. I can't get a straight answer out of him, much less a commitment.

MADELINE. Well what did I tell you about dating cops? In the five years I've know her, she's dated three cops.

JANE. Yeah, can't you give a fireman a chance? They're a lot more reliable. You know where they are half the time, and they learn how to cook at the firehouse.

LORETTA. I don't know, it doesn't really feel the same. Cops are so forceful, so…I don't know…

ALLISON. Dangerous?

LORETTA. Yeah, that's it. Why, did you ever date a policeman?

ALLISON. No, but my sister is married to one.

LORETTA. Really? Maybe Frank knows him. What's his name?

ALLISON. Bret Baxter… You see my sister and I used to double date a lot before we opened the beauty salon.

LORETTA. No kidding? Unisex?

ALLISON. No, we just dated men, but, whatever floats your boat.

MADELINE. What's the name of your shop?

ALLISON. *(now proud of the clever name)* "Hair Apparent."

JANE. "Hair Apparent," *(nodding to* **MADELINE***)* "Hair Apparent." I don't get it?

ALLISON. Neither do I.

LORETTA. Well, I know what I get. *(She removes the pillow from her bag.)* A big pain in the neck from a big fathead cop I'm *allegedly* dating. He goes down to Atlantic City with his buddies for the weekend then comes back and has the nerve to ask me if he can borrow for the rent. Like I'm made of money or something. *(hits pillow)* I'm living paycheck to paycheck as it is. Ohhh, he really pisses me off. I think I need a smoke.

(She pulls out a pack of cigarettes.)

ALLISON. Well, you see, there's your problem.

LORETTA. What do you mean?

ALLISON. The cigarettes.

LORETTA. Hey, I don't think I need a lecture from you honey, my cardiologist is doing just fine.

ALLISON. I'm not even referring to your health, which is a real concern. I'm talking about your lack of money problem.

LORETTA. I'm not following you.

ALLISON. How many packs a day do you smoke?

LORETTA. Oh, not much, maybe a half.

MADELINE. *(correcting her)* Maybe two and a half.

*(***LORETTA*** *shoots* **MADELINE** *a look.)*

ALLISON. Okay, we'll say it's a pack and a half. At ten-fifty a pack, adjusting for inflation... *(She starts doing the math with her hand as if writing on a blackboard.)* That's sixteen-fifty times three hundred and sixty-five days. Let's see, carry the five and add the...

LORETTA. Six thousand twenty-two dollars and fifty cents. You're not the first one who's told me.

JANE. You spend close to six thousand on cigarettes?

MADELINE. Don't even get her started on the three cups of Starbuck's coffee she drinks a day.

ALLISON. There you go. How much for a latte? Three, four bucks a cup, *(back to math)* times three a day, carry the eight, divide by three…

LORETTA. *(exasperated)* All right, all right, I get the point. Are we here discuss to my net worth or bash men?

CECELIA. *(offstage)* No, Mother, I cannot help you sauté the cous-cous, the almonds will have to wait… I have my own nuts, I mean, patients waiting.

(Group reacts as CECELIA enters.)

I'm sorry I'm late, ladies. Oh, I see you've met our new member, Allison.

ALLISON. Yes, they have! And I really think I'm bonding with the group.

LORETTA. Like crazy glue.

CECELIA. I have some very good news, people! With the remainder of tonight's session we are going to resume our 'role playing' therapy.

JANE. You mean you found someone?

CECELIA. That's what I'm saying. He should be here shortly. But first, did anyone give any thought to our assignment from last week?

(No reaction from the group.)

No one? Oh, I'm sorry Allison, you're new. Our assignment last week was to try and come up with some words or catchphrase that might help us when we're struggling to cope with our relationships. And I'm not talking about the standard clichés like "he doesn't deserve you" or "you can do much better." I'm talking about something a little more empowering!

(Again, silence from the group.)

Come now ladies, someone must have come up with something?

(More silence as ALLISON excitedly raises her hand.)

ALLISON. Ohh, ohh! Well, when I was a cheerleader in high school…

LORETTA. *(sarcasm evident)* You were a cheerleader…there's a surprise.

CECELIA. *(scolding)* LORETTA!

ALLISON. Well, anyway, when one of us would break up with a guy, we used to sing this little song to cheer us up.

CECELIA. Oh, a little ditty?

ALLISON. No, a little song.

CECELIA. What's it called?

ALLISON. Men Are Dogs.

CECELIA. I wanted to call my book that.

ALLISON. What a coincidence…or is it a play on words?

CECELIA. Why don't you let us hear it?

ALLISON. All right, it's sung the same as "Row, Row, Row Your Boat." I'll start, and you can all join in.

MADELINE. I can't wait.

ALLISON. *(starts to sing and does arm movements as if leading a cheer)* Men, men, men are dogs, sad but it is true…You meet 'em, you date 'em, you love 'em, you hate 'em… what are we to do?

(She repeats and motions for them to join in which they ignore.)

ALLISON. *(to DOCTOR MONAHAN)* Can I get a little help here?

CECELIA. Come now, ladies. Let's give it a try. Use your pillows.

(ALLISON continues as ladies reluctantly start then get more emotional with each repeated verse, constantly hitting their respective pillows… By the fifth time, TONY stands dumbfounded in entry listening and reacting to a few choruses of the song.)

CECELIA. That's enough, ladies. Mr. Rumson has arrived.

(They all throw their pillows at him.)

TONY. Hi, Doctor Monahan. Is this the group?

CECELIA. This is it. Ladies, I'd like you to meet Tony Rumson. He's the person I told you about who's going to participate in our group tonight.

*(Silence from group as all but **ALLISON** glare at him.)*

TONY. *(to **CECELIA**)* Seem a bit hostile, don't they?

CECELIA. Nonsense. They just need to warm up to you. Now, group, it's time for our 'role playing' therapy. In this first scene, we will deal with a couple who have been dating for three months and are now having a nice dinner out at a casual dining establishment. Madeline, I'd like you to play opposite Mr. Rumson. Now, let's get everything set up.

(They place small table down center with two chairs on either side.)

TONY. *(extends his hand, which she ignores)* I'm Tony.

MADELINE. *(coldly)* You sit there.

(She indicates chair and they each sit.)

CECELIA. Now, who would like to play the waitress?

ALLISON. I will.

CECELIA. All right. Allison is the waitress. Let's begin.

TONY. But, what do I do?

CECELIA. Just try to act like you normally would if you'd been dating someone for three months.

TONY. But, you've got to give me more than that. I mean, how'd we meet, have we slept together?

CECELIA. Have you ever dated anyone for three months and not slept with her, Mr. Rumson? *(whispers directions to **ALLISON**)*

TONY. I get your point. Okay, I'm ready. *(to **MADELINE**)* So, nice place, hey babe?

MADELINE. Compared to what? But, it only stands to reason. I mean, what could I expect after three months? Do you remember our first date? You took me to dinner and a show. You brought me flowers and candy...and now, three short months later, this dump.

TONY. *(To* **CECELIA.***)* Hey, what is this?

CECELIA. It's therapy, Mr. Rumson. Just go with the flow.

TONY. Whatever you say. *(back to* **MADELINE***)* This place isn't so bad, baby. Let's order something. *(He calls to* **ALLISON.***)* Waitress.

MADELINE. How romantic, always thinking about your stomach.

*(***ALLISON*** comes wiggling over with a sexy stride, as instructed by* **DR. MONAHAN.***)*

ALLISON. *(speaks to* **TONY** *in breathy, sexy voice)* I'm Allison, your waitress. Would you like to look at a menu or do you just want to see... *(shakes her cleavage at* **TONY.***)* The special.

TONY. *(trying unsuccessfully to ignore* **ALLISON***)* Menu, specials, whatever.

MADELINE. Why don't you just bring us some water for the time being, I think he needs to cool off.

ALLISON. *(normal voice)* Sure thing, sweetie.

(She leaves to get water.)

MADELINE. Take a picture next time.

TONY. What are you talking about?

MADELINE. I saw the way you were coming on to her.

TONY. I didn't say two words.

MADELINE. *(imitating* **ALLISON,** *she emphasizes by cupping her breasts in her hands)* "Would you like to see the specials", what was that all about?

TONY. What do I know? We're here trying to have a nice dinner, the waitress comes over and all of a sudden, I'm having an affair with her?

MADELINE. So, you ARE having an affair with her. I knew it. And you tell me today of all days?

TONY. I am not having an affair with the waitress, and what is 'today of all days.'

MADELINE. June eleventh. Ring a bell?

TONY. Flag Day?

MADELINE. It's our three-month anniversary.

TONY. It is?

MADELINE. Don't you remember when we met at that tennis mixer?

TONY. I don't even play tennis.

MADELINE. Then what were you doing at the mixer?

TONY. How the hell do I know? Trying to pick up women, probably.

MADELINE. It figures, typical man. What am I, just another notch on your bedpost till you sucker the next unsuspecting female?

TONY. Now, just calm down a second, will you baby?

MADELINE. Don't you "baby" me. This isn't the first time I've caught you looking at another woman.

TONY. *(to* **CECILIA***)* Alright, this is getting to be a little too much.

(**ALLISON** *walks over with two cups of water.*)

ALLISON. *(to* **TONY***)* Here's your water, tiger. *(She puts cups down on table.)* We still on for next week baby?

MADELINE. You two-timing bastard.

(She throws one cup of water in his face and the second at his crotch.)

TONY. *(to* **CECELIA** *as he rises)* That's it, I've had enough.

CECELIA. *(She goes to* **TONY** *and begins to dry him off.)* Aw, come now, Tony. Is a little water going to discourage you? Besides, remember what I'm paying you.

TONY. Alright, I'll stay.

CECELIA. Great. Okay, next vignette. Loretta, front and center. You two have been married ten years and you're having a quiet evening sitting home watching TV…Ready?

*(***TONY** *and* **LORETTA** *move to the chairs.* **TONY***, afraid now to upset her, watches her feign sitting first and pops up a few times, countering, until she finally watches him sit first and smiles as she sits last, showing her dominance.)*

CECELIA. Go.

LORETTA. *(extremely shrill tone)* Oh, no you don't. You're not watching football again. *Desperate Housewives* is on.

TONY. *(a little more tentative)* It's a re-run?

LORETTA. I don't care. Give me that remote.

TONY. Here, take it.

(He pretends to hand her the remote.)

LORETTA. So, anything interesting happen down at the station house lately?

TONY. I'm a cop?

LORETTA. No, you're a brain surgeon, of course you're a cop. What, do you have Alzheimer's?

TONY. I don't know anymore.

LORETTA. Well you must have Alzheimer's because you're forgetting to hide the love letters from your girlfriends.

(She stands up.)

TONY. What letters? What girlfriends?

LORETTA. Don't try to weasel your way out of this one, you son of a bitch.

(She shoves him off chair and he falls to stage.)

TONY. *(to* **CECELIA***)* This is ridiculous!

LORETTA. Here, I'll read it to you. *(She pretends to read letter as she slowly backs him behind sofa.)* My dearest, dearest darling. I can't wait till we're together again. I know you told me you can't stand living with that shrew one more moment.

TONY. This has gone far enough!

LORETTA. Shrew am I? I'll show you who's a shrew, you creep.

(She punches him in the stomach then in the face causing him to fall behind the couch out of sight of audience. She stomps on him a few times for emphasis.)

I want you out of my house. Out, do you hear?!!

(**TONY** *remains hidden behind sofa as* **CECELIA** *pulls* **LORETTA** *stage right.* **LORETTA** *breaks from* **CECELIA** *and goes back to give* **TONY** *one more kick.*)

CECELIA. *(to* **LORETTA**) Deep breaths, deep breaths.

(**LORETTA** *clasps her hands together and brings them slowly down from above her head to her stomach as she takes deep breath. [Optional: she runs back to give him one more before* **CECELIA** *again separates them.])*

TONY. *(slowly raises his hand from behind couch until he is fully visible)* That does it. Money or no money, I'm out of here.

(He runs out door.)

CECELIA. *(crossing after him)* Wait, Tony, don't leave. We haven't finished the session yet. *(She yells out door.)* So I'll see you tomorrow night? Okay, go ahead and run then. Typical man, when things get a little tough they leave you flat.

JANE. But I didn't get to go yet, doctor?

CECELIA. I'm sorry, Jane. You can go first next time...Now, ladies, doesn't everyone feel better?

(They all answer, "Yes, Doctor Monahan," etc. as curtain falls on Act I.)

LORETTA. I know I do!

(curtain)

ACT II

Scene One

(Setting: CECELIA's office. One week later.)

(At rise: CECELIA is sitting on her chair besides sofa where Jane is lying.)

CECELIA. As you know Jane, the most important part of therapy is coming to grips with your past relationships. Now it's been a while since you dated anyone and we have to try to reconcile why you have this apprehension about starting a new relationship.

JANE. I understand, Doctor Monahan. I just don't know why I'm so afraid to date.

CECELIA. Tell me about your last relationship...it was how long ago?

JANE. Two years.

CECELIA. So it's been two years since you've been with a man?

JANE. *(A little embarrassed.)* Oh, were you just talking about men? Make it five years.

CECELIA. I'm sorry, Jane. I didn't realize.

JANE. Look, it only happened once, we were both drunk and lonely. I shouldn't even count it.

CECELIA. Okay, let's confine this to your relationships with men, shall we?

JANE. I think that's a good idea...yeah, okay, just men.

CECELIA. Fine. Now five years ago you went out with a man named?

JANE. Floyd.

CECELIA. Floyd. Okay, tell me about Floyd.

JANE. He was very exciting, and mysterious.

CECELIA. And what was the problem? Did he mistreat you? Ignore you?

JANE. Not at all, doctor. He was one of the most attentive, wonderful, passionate men I've ever met.

CECELIA. You caught him cheating on you, then.

JANE. Floyd? Never, he wasn't the type. Besides, he was crazy about me. The times I spent with him were some of the best memories of my life.

CECELIA. Then I don't see what the problem was.

JANE. That's just it, Dr., I had wonderful times when I was with him, but after a while I was hardly ever with him.

CECELIA. Why not?

JANE. I guess it was because he worked mainly nights and I worked days.

CECELIA. Lots of couples work different shifts and still manage to maintain a healthy relationship. In fact because they have limited time for each other, it sometimes makes their time together even more special.

JANE. I know, that's how it was for us.

CECELIA. What business was he in?

JANE. *(pause)* Ah…banking.

CECELIA. Come on, Jane, you're an intelligent woman, you know bankers work nine to five. He was a banker who worked nights? What really happened?

JANE. *(embarrassed)* Okay, I found out later that the reason he had to work nights was because…he was robbing the banks!

CECELIA. You were dating a bank robber and you didn't know it?

JANE. He was pretty closed-mouthed about his work. I'd ask him how his night went and he would just tell me it was profitable.

CECELIA. So what happened to him?

JANE. That's the funny part, Dr. If I'd have stayed with him it would have been the perfect relationship. I'd know where my boyfriend was all the time.

CECELIA. He's in jail, isn't he?

JANE. Two to six in Leavenworth, but with good behavior he'll be out in six months. Do you think I should start things up with him again?

CECELIA. You're not serious? Are you?

JANE. Why not? He didn't drink, smoke or take drugs. He was in great shape and terrific in the sack.

CECELIA. And, I imagine he was a good provider.

JANE. *(after a thought)* Yeah, that too.

CECELIA. Still, I think you'd better put that relationship to rest and try to move on now.

JANE. I guess you're right, doctor.

CECELIA. Well, time's up Jane, I'll see you tonight in group.

JANE. Alright Dr. Monahan. I'll see you tonight. Are we doing role playing again?

CECELIA. I don't think Mr. Rumson will be coming back, and unless I can find a replacement for him...oh, but where would I find someone on such short notice?

(BOB enters with a package.)

BOB. Hello, Dr. Monahan.

CECELIA. Oh, Hello Bob.

BOB. I'm sorry, you're with someone, I'll come back later.

CECELIA. That's quite alright, Bob. Jane was just leaving.

JANE. *(aside to CECELIA)* You think he can take a punch?

CECELIA. Goodbye, Jane. I'll see you tonight.

JANE. Alright, I'm going, I'm going. *(to BOB)* See you later.

(She exits.)

CECELIA. Is that package for me?

BOB. Oh yes it is, Dr. Monahan.

CECELIA. Why don't you sit down for a second? You must get tired delivering those packages.

BOB. Thanks, I could use a little break. Aren't you going to open your package?

CECELIA. Not right now. *(She puts package on desk.)* Bob, I wanted to ask you something but I don't want to seem forward.

BOB. Please, be as forward as you like.

CECELIA. Are you busy tonight?

BOB. Not especially, what did you have in mind?

CECELIA. Tell me, were you very athletic in school?

BOB. This is certainly getting interesting. As a matter of fact I ran track and played a little ice hockey.

CECELIA. Ice hockey, huh. That's a pretty physical sport. I guess you can take a little punishment then, huh Bob?

BOB. I've been rolled around a bit. What did you have in mind, a romantic dinner, maybe a movie and then back to my place?

CECELIA. Well, I really think I could use your services tonight.

BOB. But, Cecelia, I hardly know you! Ah, what the hell? What time tonight? Should I bring the wine?

CECELIA. Seven thirty and you can skip the wine. And Bob...

BOB. Yes, Cecelia.

CECELIA. I pay sixty dollars an hour.

BOB. You're going to pay me? I don't know if I like that idea. But hey, if it will make you feel better.

CECELIA. Bob, pay attention for a second. I'm paying you to help with the women in my group.

BOB. Group. How many are in it?

CECELIA. Four.

BOB. I don't know, two's usually my limit, but maybe if I go home and take a nap for an hour...drink a Red Bull...

CECELIA. Bob, you don't understand, this is therapy.

BOB. Hey, call it whatever the hell you want! You might need a bigger couch though.

CECELIA. Not sexual therapy, Bob. Just plain old therapy, group therapy. Now are you game? You'd really be helping me out a lot.

BOB. Cecelia, if I'm helping you out in any way I'd be happy to do it.

CECELIA. Excellent. I'll see you tonight then.

BOB. Tonight it is.

(He exits as **ROSE** *comes in from interior entrance.)*

ROSE. Cecelia, I can't believe you tricked that poor man into helping you with your group.

CECELIA. Mother, have you been eavesdropping on my private conversations?

ROSE. I was doing laundry.

CECELIA. Then how are you privy to my conversations?

ROSE. The vent in the corner of your office connects to the laundry room.

CECELIA. Isn't that a nice revelation. And for your information, I did not trick Bob into helping. He was glad to do it.

ROSE. You know why, don't you?

CECELIA. Probably for the money, like all the rest.

ROSE. Nonsense, he's doing it because he's attracted to you.

CECELIA. That's absurd.

ROSE. It's true.

CECELIA. How would you know?

ROSE. Just a mother's intuition.

CECELIA. Just what did you and Bob talk about the other day, Mother?

ROSE. *(evasive)* Just casual conversation. Say, Cecelia, did you ever find that bottle of sherry around here?

CECELIA. Stop trying to change the subject, Mother. Now what happened with you and Bob?

ROSE. We just talked, nothing personal, well, maybe I mentioned what a bum your father was, but other than that.

CECELIA. You had no right to discuss family matters with a stranger, Mother.

ROSE. Why not? You do it all the time.

CECELIA. That's different and you know it.

ROSE. Why?

CECELIA. *(a little flustered)* Because, because...I get paid to do it, that's why. Now if you don't mind I'm very busy.

ROSE. Alright, I'm going. *(She starts for door.)*

CECELIA. And one more thing, Mother.

ROSE. What's that?

CECELIA. I want you to promise me you'll never eavesdrop on another private conversation of mine again.

ROSE. Starting when?

CECELIA. Starting now, Mother.

ROSE. Alright, alright. It's not like I'll ever hear a better story than that woman who dated the bank robber anyway.

CECELIA. Mother!

ROSE. But I want you to make me a promise too, Cecelia.

CECELIA. And what's that?

ROSE. Well, since you won't call the dentist, promise you'll give that Bob a fair chance. He seems like a decent guy.

CECELIA. I'll give it some thought.

ROSE. Coming from you, that's practically a concession.

CECELIA. Well, I have some errands to run before this evening's session.

ROSE. Alright. Do you mind if I look around down here one more time for the sherry.

CECELIA. Okay. But stay away from my files! I don't want my privacy invaded again. And I'll ask you to stop doing the laundry during office hours.

ROSE. And when would you like me to do it. At midnight?

CECELIA. Tell me something. Why doesn't the noise from the washing machine cover up my conversations? ?

ROSE. Oh it does. But when I'm first in there loading the… and I hear something juicy, I just load a little slower.

CECELIA. Well, I'm putting you on your honor to load a little faster. I'll see you later.

(**CECELIA** *gathers her purse and jacket and moves towards exterior door.*)

ROSE. Oh by the way honey, do you mind if we skip breakfast tomorrow? *(coyly)* I might not be home.

CECELIA. Really, where will you be?

ROSE. *(excited)* I've got a date tonight.

CECELIA. A date? With whom?

ROSE. Angelo! That fella from cooking class I told you about. I'm baking a special dessert that I'm bringing over to him. Then he's taking me to dinner and then back to his place for dessert and if I read things right, well, you never know. Carpe Diem!

CECELIA. Mother! Don't tell me *you're* the dessert! And on the first date? I thought you told me you were too old?

ROSE. Hey. When you get to be my age you don't wait around to be pinned at the debutante ball. If the mood strikes you…bingo!

CECELIA. Bingo?

ROSE. Bingo.

CECELIA. I have to get going. We'll talk more about bingo when I get home! *(She exits.)*

ROSE. *(starts singing as she exits:)* B-I-N-G-O, B-I-N-G-O, B-I-N-G-O AND BINGO WAS HIS NAME-O!

(blackout)

Scene Two

(Setting: Same as before, early evening.)

(At rise: **CECELIA** *enters main door. She is on her cell phone.)*

CECELIA. No Paula, valium is not a substitute for therapy. Where did you hear a thing like that?…Oh, Mom, huh? *(crosses to desk)* Listen Sis, how about she comes to live with you for a while?…Why not?…Paula, you've been painting that guest room ever since she moved in with me…*(sits behind desk)* No, I haven't called that dentist yet and stop changing the subject, you're as bad as Mom…

*(***ROSE*** enters interior door dressed for her date.)*

ROSE. Who's that, Cecelia?

CECELIA. Your other daughter.

ROSE. *(loudly to phone)* You mean the one who never invites me to stay overnight!

CECELIA. *(to phone)* Hello… Paula? You still there? …That did it! She hung up.

ROSE. *(twirling to show off her dress)* Ah, the truth hurts. I think she should be your patient.

CECELIA. *(rising)* Speaking of which, they will be arriving shortly so I have to get ready.

ROSE. And I have to finish getting ready for my date with Angelo!

CECELIA. You look very pretty. But I want you to be careful. Did you give any more thought to what we discussed?

ROSE. Regarding?

CECELIA. Bingo.

ROSE. Yes, I did and I think you're absolutely right. After all, this is only our first date… I'll make him wait a day.

CECELIA. Why do I bother?

ROSE. Honestly Cecelia, for the life of me, I don't know why you don't try dating?

CECELIA. There you go again. Believe me, dating is no panacea. I get more pleasure curled up with a good book than I would wasting my time playing "what's your sign?" with some obnoxious cad. And, probably, with just one thing on his mind.

ROSE. Well, if he had the right equipment...

CECELIA. What are you saying?

ROSE. Well, take Angelo for instance. When he took off his apron in cooking class I noticed he had a pretty big spatula.

CECELIA. So he has a big penis. So what? That's not the be-all and end-all that makes a man.

ROSE. No, but it helps. But I suppose it means nothing to you. With your highfalutin' college degrees. You must be operating on a much higher plane than us common folk.

CECELIA. Oh, is that what you think? Well, there's where you're wrong Mom. I'd like a man with a big penis as much as the next gal. As a matter of fact, I'd love a man with a big penis. A nice, intelligent, sensitive, gentle man WITH A BIG PENIS!

(BOB *enters.*)

(*arms extended upward*) Please, Dear God, deliver me a man with a big penis!

BOB. Looks like your prayers have been answered.

CECELIA. Bob, you're early!

BOB. Judging from the conversation, I'd say I got here just in time.

ROSE. Hi, Bob. I was just leaving before the nuts...I mean patients get here...remember (*indicating* CECELIA *with a motion of her head*) Carpe Diem.

(ROSE *exits interior door.*)

CECELIA. Thanks for coming to help out.

BOB. My pleasure.

CECELIA. The other group members will be here shortly. Would you excuse me a second while I freshen up.

BOB. Not a problem, do you mind if I make a quick call from your phone, the battery on my cell phone died?

CECELIA. Not at all. I'll be right back.

(She exits interior door as **BOB** *dials the phone.)*

BOB. *(into phone imitating a cat)* Meoooooow, meoooow, meooow, meooow. Are you there, kitty? It's Daddy. Meooow, Meooooow,

*(***CECELIA*** re-enters.)*

Meooow, I'll be over to play with you later. Goodbye Kittty. Meooow, Meooow.

CECELIA. Who's Kitty?

BOB. Oh, that's my cat. She get's lonely when I'm not there, so I like to call my answering machine and talk to her.

CECELIA. Is that right?

*(***MADELINE*** *and* **JANE** *enter.)*

MADELINE. We're here.

CECELIA. Madeline, Jane, this is Bob Crowley.

JANE. *(in on scheme)* Yeah, we already met.

CECELIA. Bob will be helping us out with group tonight.

MADELINE. *(to* **JANE***)* I hope he's tougher than the last guy.

BOB. *(to* **CECELIA***)* What does she mean?

CECELIA. *(to* **BOB***)* Pay no attention.

*(***ALLISON*** *enters.)*

ALLISON. Hi, everyone, I'm here.

CECELIA. Allison, I'd like you to meet our new assistant, *(catches herself)* uh...Robert Crowley.

BOB. What Robert, just call me...

*(***CECELIA*** *tries to stop him with a hand gesture.)*

Bob.

ALLISON. BOB? BOB did you say? Don't I know you from somewhere BOB?

BOB. Yeah, we met the other day, I was leaving as you were coming.

ALLISON. That's right, I remember you now Bob. Of course I didn't know your name then Bob. But I certainly noticed your thick head of hair.

(She runs her fingers through his hair.)

BOB. Really?

ALLISON. I'm in the business you know. I have my own salon, "Hair Apparent."

BOB. "Hair Apparent." Clever name!

ALLISON. If you say so. *(She starts to stroke his hair.)* Why don't you drop in for a cut sometime?

CECELIA. *(steps between them)* I think Bob needs to prepare for our session now, Allison.

*(**LORETTA** enters wearing a Hawaiian lei.)*

LORETTA. Sorry I'm late, gang. Their having a Hawaiian singles luau at the Holiday Inn. It's a real hoot. They've got a hollow log drum and roast pig and everything. I was chatting with the Ukulele player on a break and guess what his job is when he's not playing in the band?

ALL EXCEPT BOB. A cop!

LORETTA. You got it! I'm going back after tonight's group session. You guys should join me.

BOB. Not a bad idea.

LORETTA. *(coolly)* Oh, hi, I'm Loretta.

ALLISON. He's Bob.

BOB. Yes, I'm Bob, pleased to meet you.

*(**LORETTA** ignores him and sits on couch.)*

CECELIA. Well, now that we're all acquainted, I think we should get started with the session and get right into the role playing therapy.

BOB. Sounds good to me.

(**TONY** *enters, wearing dark glasses.*)

TONY. Hi everyone.

(He instinctively ducks and covers his face in anticipation of pillows being thrown then straightens up coolly when none are forthcoming.)

CECELIA. Tony, what are you doing here?

TONY. Well, I kind of felt bad running out on you like that Dr. Monahan. And I could use the money and... *(noticing* **BOB***)* Hey, who's this guy?

ALLISON. That's Bob.

CECELIA. Enough Allison. Tony, I'm surprised to see you after what you went through.

BOB. *(to* **JANE** *and* **LORETTA***)* What did he go through?

TONY. Call me crazy, but I was kind of starting to enjoy it. *(takes off glasses to reveal black eye)*

CECELIA. Well as long as you're here. Why don't you sit down and observe. Bob is going to role-play with the group tonight.

TONY. Wait a minute. You mean to tell me that *this guy* is going to role-play with...*them?*

CECELIA. That's what I'm saying.

TONY. Oh, I can't wait to see this! *(anxious)* Would you like me to help you set up?

CECELIA. That would be great Mr. Rumson.

*(***TONY***, chuckling to himself, sets up two chairs with no table this time downstage. He then finds a seat and sits to observe. He reacts accordingly in the background to all going on.)*

CECELIA. Now Bob, you and Jane have been dating for about a year and she discovers a secret about you.

BOB. Sounds great, let's give it a try.

CECELIA. Start it off, Jane.

JANE. *(hesitant to participate)* Oh, I don't know if I can.

CECELIA. Come on, you can do it.

JANE. *(meekly)* Okay.

> *(JANE and BOB both sit as JANE once again looks at CECILIA who nods her head in encouragement.)*

Why didn't you tell me you were a damned bank robber!

> *(BOB, taken aback, looks at TONY who only smiles at him and nods his head.)*

BOB. *(thinking on his feet)* Sweetheart, I only kept it a secret from you because I didn't want to *hurt* you. I told you I wasn't able to finish college because I had to support my mother and...two baby sisters after my father died. And you're so precious to me that I wanted to take you out all the time and buy you nice things.

JANE. *(She's won over.)* Oh, Bob.

BOB. *(a quick glance to TONY as he starts laying it on)* Don't you see honey, without you my life is meaningless. But if it makes *you* happy, I'll give up the bank heists and get a good honest job. One you'll be proud of. Because the only thing that's important to me is your happiness.

CECELIA. *(not buying it)* Oh Bob!

ALLISON. Oh Bob!

JANE. *(swooning)* That's so beautiful.

TONY. *(from chair)* She would have punched ME.

BOB. *(standing)* Next.

CECELIA. *(now pulling out the big guns)* Loretta, front and center!

> *(LORETTA stands.)*

You're sitting at home *watching* TV *with your husband.*

> *(TONY laughs to himself and wags his finger as LORETTA tries to sit last but after a few false starts she pushes BOB into the chair first, then sits.)*

LORETTA. *(hostile)* Give me that remote, you're not watching football again.

BOB. *(again composed)* You're right honey, how insensitive of me. As a matter of fact there was a special on public television about… *(to* **TONY** *to show him how it's done) how to improve your relationship with your spouse (back to* **LORRETTA***)* that I was dying to watch with you. I taped it while you were sleeping because I didn't want to disturb you but I'd love if we could watch it together right now.

LORETTA. *(momentarily caught off guard)* You would? *(hostile again)* Yeah, but what about this love note I found in your jacket from your girlfriend down at the station house?

TONY. *(to his feet)* Yeah, what about that!

BOB. *(cavalierly to* **TONY***)* Oh that. You didn't take that *seriously* did you?

> *(***LORETTA** *nods.)*

You know the pressure we're under…the boys on the force always play practical jokes on each other to break the tension. We planted that same note on Clancy last week. Now don't you worry your pretty little head about a thing. You know you're the only perpetrator I want to have handcuffed to me, don't you? …Sugar?

LORETTA. Oh Bob.

ALL EXCEPT TONY & CECELIA. *(in unison)* Oh Bob.

ROSE. *(from off through vent)* Oh Bob!

> *(Everyone turns to look at vent.)*

CECELIA. Mother! Excuse me everyone…

> *(She exits.)*

MADELINE. So now what?

BOB. Well, we're supposed to be role playing. Let's think of something.

ALLISON. I know. How about we're couples double dating at a drive-in movie.

> *(She pushes* **LORETTA** *towards* **TONY***.)*

Loretta can be Tony's date.

(TONY reacts by moving his arms in a cross to ward her off as ALLISON crosses to BOB.)

And I'll be Bob's date.

MADELINE. And what about us?

ALLISON. Madeline, you can be Jane's date.

JANE. *(to MADELINE)* How'd she find out?

MADELINE. Beats me?

(They grasp each other's hands.)

LORETTA. I've got a better idea. Let's skip group tonight and go back to that Holiday Inn Luau. We'll consider it a field trip. I've got a feeling I'm going to be singing "I want to go back to my little grass shack" before the nights over.

TONY. Sounds good to me.

(TONY runs out to get away from LORETTA as all but ALLISON and BOB follow.)

ALLISON. You are coming, aren't you Bob?

BOB. Yes. But I think I better wait here so I can explain what happened to Doctor Monahan. Maybe I'll even invite her to come.

(MADELINE re-enters to drag ALLISON out.)

ALLISON. *(as she's being dragged out)* Okay, don't be long Bobby.

(BOB starts to put chairs back as CECELIA enters.)

CECELIA. So where is everyone?

BOB. Well, Cecelia I'm going to give it to you straight. They decided they had enough therapy for one evening and headed for the Holiday Inn.

CECELIA. They walked out on me?

BOB. Don't feel so bad, you can still bill them for the session.

CECELIA. Don't worry, I will.

BOB. I'm heading over to the luau too. Care to tag along?

CECELIA. Are you asking me out Bob?

BOB. Yeah, Cecelia, I guess I am. And be careful how you answer because I'm not very good at taking rejection.

CECELIA. I don't think so.

BOB. Ouch. And after what I just told you about rejection. What kind of heartless therapist are you?

CECELIA. Gee I'm sorry. I didn't think you were serious.

BOB. I wasn't. And even if I was I have no frontal lobe so I wouldn't remember, would I? So come on, how about it. It should be good for a few laughs. It's a luau, maybe they'll teach us the hula. *(He does a hula motion.)*

CECELIA. I don't think it's such a good idea. After all, my patients will be there. Although I have to admit it does sound like fun.

BOB. I think it's a great opportunity for you to observe your group in a social setting. You know, see how they interact with…'the others.'

CECELIA. By others you're referring to men, right?

BOB. You broke the code, Doctor Monahan.

CECELIA. I couldn't.

BOB. What are you going to do, hang around here and watch *Love Boat* re-reruns with Rose all night?

CECELIA. I just don't think it would be right, Bob.

BOB. Okay, but you're missing out on a great time. Guess I'll just have to dance with Alison all night.

CECELIA. You mean the 'father figure' poster child.

BOB. The very same. A few twirls around the dance floor and she'll be mine.

CECELIA. And just where did you learn how to dance?

BOB. Same place as everyone else, watching John Travolta in *Saturday Night Fever*.

(He strikes a disco pose with his finger in the air.)

CECELIA. Very impressive but I'm still not going.

BOB. You're sure now? You'd rather stay home than eat roast pig, drink exotic, frozen cocktails and dance the hula with a bunch of middle-aged singles.

CECELIA. I think so.

ROSE. *(offstage)* Cecelia would you like to help me blow torch the crème brulee?

CECELIA. I'll get my jacket.

(They both exit main door.)

(blackout)

Scene Three

(Setting: Same as before, several hours later.)

(At rise: A tipsy CECELIA and BOB enter wearing Hawaiian leis and singing "Tiny Bubbles.")

CECELIA. *(singing)* Tiny Bubbles in the wine.

BOB. *(joining her)* Tiny Bubbles, make me feel fine... *(stops singing)* Hey, how does the rest of that Cecelia go, song...I mean how does the rest of the song go, Cecelia?

CECELIA. Beats the hell out of me!

(They both resume singing the same two lines a few times.)

BOB. Wait, wait I'm tired of that one. Let's sing another...I got it...wait... oops... I forget it.

CECELIA. Oh, Bobby, Bobby...I learned a new one the other day in group!

BOB. No kiddin'? The glory girls taught you a song. What's it called?

CECELIA. Get this Bobby, Bobby. It's called 'Men are Dogs.' Is that a hoot or what?

(She slaps his shoulder and he falls to the couch as she plops next to him.)

BOB. No kiddin?

CECELIA. No kiddin Bobby...so, you wanna hear it?

BOB. Hear what?

CECELIA. The song I learned from the glory girls.

BOB. Yeah, yeah, let's hear it?

CECELIA. Okay...you start it and I'll join in....no, wait, that's not right...*you* start it and *I'll* join in.

BOB. Okay go ahead.

CECELIA. Okay I will. *(She starts to sing but can't remember correctly.)* Men are dogs, Men are dogs...that is what I mean...blah, bla, blah bla, blah, bla, blah...life is but a dream. Okay...now sing with me...

(They both start to sing.)

Shush, shush Bobby shhh *(points to ceiling)* we have to be quiet. Rose is sleeping.

BOB. Rose is upstairs sleeping?

CECELIA. She better be... Hey Bobby, you know what? We had a lot of fun tonight. You know, for a guy with no frontal lobe you're alright.

BOB. Thanks, Cecelia.

CECELIA. *(removing his lei)* Ya like me, don't ya Bobby?

BOB. *(removing her lei)* Yeah, I guess I do...Ohh, ohh that reminds me. Did ya open it yet?

CECELIA. Open what?

BOB. The package I delivered to you?

CECELIA. Nah, it's sittin on the table in my room, why?

BOB. It's a surprise.

CECELIA. It is? How would you know?

BOB. I know because I heard ya liked surprises.

CECELIA. Did you send that package to me, Bobby?

BOB. Sure did.

CECELIA. But why?

BOB. I told ya, because I heard ya liked surprises.

CECELIA. *(She slaps him on the back again.)* My, but aren't you the charmer Bobby!

BOB. Ya know something. I'm gonna let you in on a little secret.

CECELIA. Yeah? What's that?

BOB. I didn't always do this job.

CECELIA. No kiddin?

BOB. No, no, no siree, Marie. I was the editor of the college newspaper.

CECELIA. You wanted to be a writer?

BOB. Even better, a playwright. You bet. And I wrote some too, even got one produced upstate but...the powers that be stopped me, Cecelia.

CECELIA. Ohh, I hate them. Who were they?

BOB. They weren't a who, they were a they, everyone. My parents, *(can't pronounce following word)* my sibilingings, my sibilingings…my brothers and sisters.

CECELIA. So what'd ya do?

BOB. I got a job as a school teacher.

CECELIA. You were a teacher, Bobby?

BOB. You were! So was I.

CECELIA. No kiddin', what subject did you teach?

BOB. American History.

CECELIA. That's how ya knew about the Native Americans, isn't it.

BOB. That's right. All I wanted to do was teach history and write plays. Now where's the harm in that.

CECELIA. Exactly.

BOB. But then the powers that be got me. Hey Celia. Did you always want to be a psycomotrist… psycolockagist, a shrink?

CECELIA. Heck no.

BOB. You didn't? So what did you always want to be?

CECELIA. Do you really want to know?

BOB. Sure do!

CECELIA. A playwright! *(She starts to laugh.)*

BOB. Oh you're just foolin me, aren't you.

CECELIA. Yeah, I'm just foolin you, Bobby.

BOB. No, c'mon! Tell me Celia, in your heart of hearts, what did you always want to be?

CECELIA. Promise you won't laugh?

BOB. Cross my heart.

CECELIA. Well, ever since I was a little girl I always wanted to be a dancer.

BOB. I knew you liked to dance. You cut a mean rug at that Luau. How'd you learn how to dance so good?

(She rises from couch and demonstrates.)

CECELIA. Well, when I was a little girl, and my daddy would come home from an early gig, he would always take my hands and put my feet up on his feet, and we'd dance and dance. And ever since then I wanted to be a dancer.

BOB. *(in front of couch)* But Cecelia, if you always wanted to be a dancer then why didn't you become one?

CECELIA. I wasn't good enough.

BOB. Oh I get it, the powers that be, right.

CECELIA. No, I just wasn't good enough.

BOB. Well anyway, even if you didn't open it, I hope you liked that I bought you a surprise.

CECELIA. Oh I do. *(She moves towards the light switch.)* And guess what Bobby? I've got a surprise for you too.

BOB. Ya ,do? What is it?

(CECELIA hits the light switch and embraces BOB as they fall to the sofa.)

CECELIA. SURPRISE!

(Lights go dark.)

(No incidental music. CECELIA leaves the stage and we hear the office phone start in the black out. It rings several times as the lights come up signaling the next morning. A groggy BOB, who was sleeping on the couch, gets up to answer the phone.)

BOB. Hello...I don't know, there's no one here...what's that? You have anxiety? ...How should I know...take a valium...huh, you did already? I don't know, you better call back later. *(hangs up phone)* I need an aspirin. She's a doctor, she must have aspirin somewhere.

(He starts to look around then gives up and sits on the sofa as CECELIA, now dressed in a robe, enters interior door.)

CECELIA. So, you're up, sleeping beauty.

BOB. Well, my body is, but I think my head is stuck inside a bass drum.

CECELIA. *(She kisses his head.)* There, does that make it any better.

BOB. A little.

CECELIA. I opened your present last night. I'm very flattered that you tried to impress me.

BOB. Did you like it?

CECELIA. It was very thoughtful. I didn't think they still made lava lamps.

BOB. Isn't it neat? I found it at a novelty shop when I was upstate last week.

CECELIA. What were you doing upstate?

BOB. Visiting a relative...Hey Cecelia, last night did anything, I mean did we...

CECELIA. Get horizontal?

BOB. Well, yeah.

CECELIA. For a little while but nothing happened. You passed out.

BOB. Gee, I'm sorry.

CECELIA. Don't worry, there's always this weekend.

(She pats his head.)

BOB. OHH.

CECELIA. I'm sorry. Head still hurts, huh?

BOB. Do you have any aspirin?

CECELIA. You just have to know where to look. Mother keeps the medicine on a high shelf in the laundry room. *(She starts to exit as phone rings. From doorway.)* Would you mind getting that, just take a message.

(She exits.)

BOB. Hello, Dr. Monahan's office. *(pause)* Kitty! Is that you. *(He moves with cordless receiver downstage under the vent to get away from interior door.)* This is a real bad time babe. Hey, How'd you get this number? The caller I.D.? *(aside)* Damn... No, I wasn't cursing at you babe. *(pause)* This is one of the stops on my route...Yes, of course I love you, baby...Look, I really have to go...I'll see you Sunday...Okay...kiss the kids for me, Bye.

(He hangs up phone and sits back down on couch as
CECELIA *re-appears in the doorway.)*

CECELIA. *(from behind him with false sincerity)* Bobby sweetie.
Does your head still hurt?

BOB. It hurts bad, baby.

CECELIA. Well, the Doctor has a home made remedy that's
gonna fix you right up. Now you just close your eyes
and I'll deliver it personally.

BOB. Now there's a switch. You're going to deliver
something to me.

CECELIA. Are you ready, baby?

BOB. I'm ready baby, lay it on me!

*(***CECELIA*** pours water over his head as he jumps from
sofa.)*

BOB. What the hell do you call this remedy!

CECELIA. A new frontal lobe, KITTY!

BOB. What do you have, super hearing?

CECELIA. No a nosy mother with a pipeline to the laundry
room.

BOB. You know there's a good explanation for this.

CECELIA. Save it, pal. We're both too old for games. You
told me you were single.

BOB. I told you I didn't have a girlfriend.

CECELIA. You also told me you were divorced!

BOB. I am, from my first wife.

CECELIA. You have a second wife?

BOB. We're separated!

CECELIA. Since when?

BOB. Since I came down from upstate and took this job.
Now I only go back every Wednesday and Sunday.

CECELIA. Just answer me one question. Why? Why go
through the trouble? The charade?

BOB. Because I liked you.

CECELIA. And you don't like you're wife and kids?

BOB. Of course, I do. I...I...I guess I'm just a...

CECELIA. A commitment phobic infidel.

BOB. That's kind of a harsh way to put it.

CECELIA. Figures, you're just a creep like the rest of them.

BOB. What's your problem, Doc? Nothing happened. We had a little harmless fun and you're making it out to be *Love Story*. We didn't even sleep together.

CECELIA. No, but we easily could have. Or are you going to tell me you would have been noble enough to contain yourself? Just what is with you guys? What makes you think you can just use women like dish rags?

BOB. Contain myself? You kissed me first, remember. And I didn't use you, Cecelia. It's not always about women. Maybe men have too much emotional baggage, or are scared, or have just been in a relationship one too many times.

CECELIA. Well at least you didn't blame your mother. Now I think you ought to leave. Unless there are anymore games you want to play?

BOB. I'm playing games? And what about you? Isn't that what you do when you role-play in therapy? You're just upset because I know how to play the game so well. It's what relationships are all about. You women are conditioned to have a perception of what the perfect man should be and the guy who can play the part best wins the prize. Well, I've got news for you, *Doctor*, no man could live up to those ideals for very long. There's no such thing as a knight in shining in armor who'll whisk you away to a castle and take care of you the rest of your life. Everyone has to take care of themselves! You of all people should know that!

CECELIA. Oh, I know that all too well. Relationships are work. Hard work. But what would that mean to a "player" like you.

BOB. At least I'm in the game. I'm not running off to my room to bury myself in a manuscript.

(BOB and CECELIA's next two lines may overlap in the heat of conversation.)

God, Cecelia, even your patients, with all their miserable experiences, still put themselves out there.

CECELIA. You are in no position to make judgments about my patients or me.

(a beat)

BOB. Look, I thought...I *know* there was something between us.

CECELIA. Whatever you think you know is based on a lie, Bob. Because everything about you is a lie. There is *nothing* between us. Now if you don't mind.

(BOB starts to exit...from doorway.)

BOB. So I guess sex this weekend is out of the question, huh?

CECELIA. Get out. Don't come back.

(BOB exits as CECELIA picks up the lies, throws them to the floor, and then sits on the sofa and sobs silently a few beats. ROSE comes in behind her and kisses her on the head.)

CECELIA. You heard, Mom?

ROSE. I did. I'm sorry, honey.

(She crosses to desk to get box of tissues then sits next to CECELIA.)

CECELIA. Well I'm not. Better I find out right away.

ROSE. If it makes you feel any better, he kind of charmed me a little, too.

CECELIA. It doesn't make me feel any better, but thanks.

(CECELIA again starts to sob softly as ROSE hands her a tissue.)

ROSE. What's the matter honey? You hardly knew the man.

CECELIA. It's not him, Mom. It's just that...that...

ROSE. What sweety?

CECELIA. There's just something wrong. Something terribly wrong with me…with my life.

ROSE. What could be wrong hon? You have a great career, money, I don't understand why you're so upset.

CECELIA. There's just something missing, Mom. I don't know, it's hard for me to express it. Can you believe that? Me, the therapist, the person with all the answers.

ROSE. Nobody has all the answers honey. You're a human being.

CECELIA. But they want me to, Mom. These women, they come to me with these expectations that what I tell them will cure their loneliness. Like I have a magic wand I can wave that will make all their pain disappear. I'm not their fairy godmother.

ROSE. Of course you're not, Cecelia. And that's not your job. You're there to help them cope with their relationship problems, that's all.

CECELIA. Help them cope. That's a laugh! If they only knew. Boy, if they only knew.

ROSE. Knew what Cecelia?

CECELIA. That I'm as lonely as they are, Mommy!

ROSE. I know, honey. And I'm sorry.

CECELIA. Since Ted died I just haven't been able to… we were so right for each other, always on the same wavelength…and to have him taken from me so suddenly.

ROSE. Your father left me after just three years of marriage honey, and I managed okay.

CECELIA. That was different, Mom. You could have reconciled with Daddy, worked on things. What choice did I have?

ROSE. Is that what you think? That I had a choice. You think it's easier for me because your father didn't die? At least you had closure. And you know your husband really loved you…

CECELIA. Well maybe if you had been more supportive of him…

ROSE. *(up from couch)* Supportive of him?! Listen to yourself, Cecelia...He had two little girls here. *This* is where he should have been, supporting us! But he made his choice, he lived his life, and now you have to bury the past and start living yours.

CECELIA. And how do I do that Mom?

ROSE. Persevere, Cecelia. If you want anything in life you have to persevere. It's how you became a therapist, isn't it? You say you're lonely, then go on the internet and meet men. Date one a month until you find a good one.

(She sits next to her.)

CECELIA. Funny that you're giving me advice on relationships.

ROSE. Sometimes no matter how much you think you know you have to hear it from someone else. Take control of your life, Cecelia. Isn't that what you'd tell your patients? Be proactive. Unless you expect "Prince Charming" to just come waltzing in the door?"

(They both look towards the front door.)

CECELIA. No, I guess not.

ROSE. So what are you going to do now, Cecelia?

CECELIA. Persevere Mom, persevere.

ROSE. Well, I've got laundry to do, sweetie.

(ROSE kisses CECELIA's cheek and exits. CECELIA crosses to her desk and dials her cell phone.)

CECELIA. Hello, Paula. Okay, text me his number. Yes, the dentist! Yes, I will let you know how it goes.

(CECELIA takes the picture of her deceased husband from her desk, gently pats it, and places it on the bookcase up back. She then picks up cordless and checks her cell for the texted number and then dials it on the cordless. She steps downstage.)

Hello Doctor Stephen Cambel? Doctor Cecelia Monahan. Yes, that's right... Good thanks. And you?

....My sister thought it might be a good idea if we got together...*(pause)* Really? Me too!....A motorcycle, how exciting!....Brand new Porsche...*(serious)* Wait a minute Stephen, can we drop the pretense? My sister said you were a nice person and I think I'm a pretty nice person. Why don't we just meet for a cup of coffee and see what happens? Saturday afternoon sounds perfect. A walk in the park sounds nice. Roller skating? Maybe...

(A violent knock at the door.)

I'm sorry Stephan, could you hold on a second... *(to door)* Who is it?

TONY. *(from off and frantic)* Tony Rumson.

CECELIA. Come in.

*(**TONY** enters panicked and disheveled. He is still wearing a lei from the night before.)*

TONY. Doctor Monahan, I need your help!

CECELIA. Tony, what's wrong?

TONY. I've got a big problem.

CECELIA. I'm on a call, Tony, but what is it?

TONY. Well, as you know, I was out with the group last night and I had a few drinks and hit the dance floor...I think you had left by then...anyway, one thing led to another and well...I woke up this morning and well...

CECELIA. Tony, what's the problem?

LORETTA. *(from doorway and dressed in a policeman's uniform)* Get back here, lover-boy! You're not getting rid of me that easy!

TONY. That's the problem Doc! You gotta help me!

*(**LORETTA** slaps a pair of handcuffs on **TONY** and starts pulling out as he ad libs.)*

Not the cuffs again!

LORETTA. And the rubber hose!

TONY. No, not the rubber hose...remember, we have a safe word...cumquat. Cumquat! Cumquat!

CECELIA. *(after them from doorway)* See you for group next Tuesday, Loretta. Bring Mr. Rumson with you. *(back to phone)* I'm sorry Stephan, patient emergency, you know how that is. Just hold another second.

(Covers phone with her hand and looks towards vent on the wall.)

Are you getting this, Mother? Listen up! *(back to phone)* So you were saying something about a walk in the park next Saturday? Just dress casually, sounds wonderful... It's a date!

ROSE. *(from off)* Carpe Diem!

(blackout)

End of Play